For Anna

Published in the United States of America by Star Bright Books, Inc., New York. The name Star Bright Books and the Star Bright Books logo are registered trademarks of Star Bright Books, Inc.

Printed in Mexico

ISBN-13: 978-1-59572-042-9

The Little Wood Duck

Brian Wildsmith

STAR BRIGHT BOOKS
NEW YORK

Once upon a time,
a mother wood duck built a nest in an old tree beside a lake. In the nest she laid six beautiful eggs.

"Come and see!
Come and see!"
she quacked.
"I'm so excited. I've laid six beautiful eggs! I have never laid so many eggs before!"

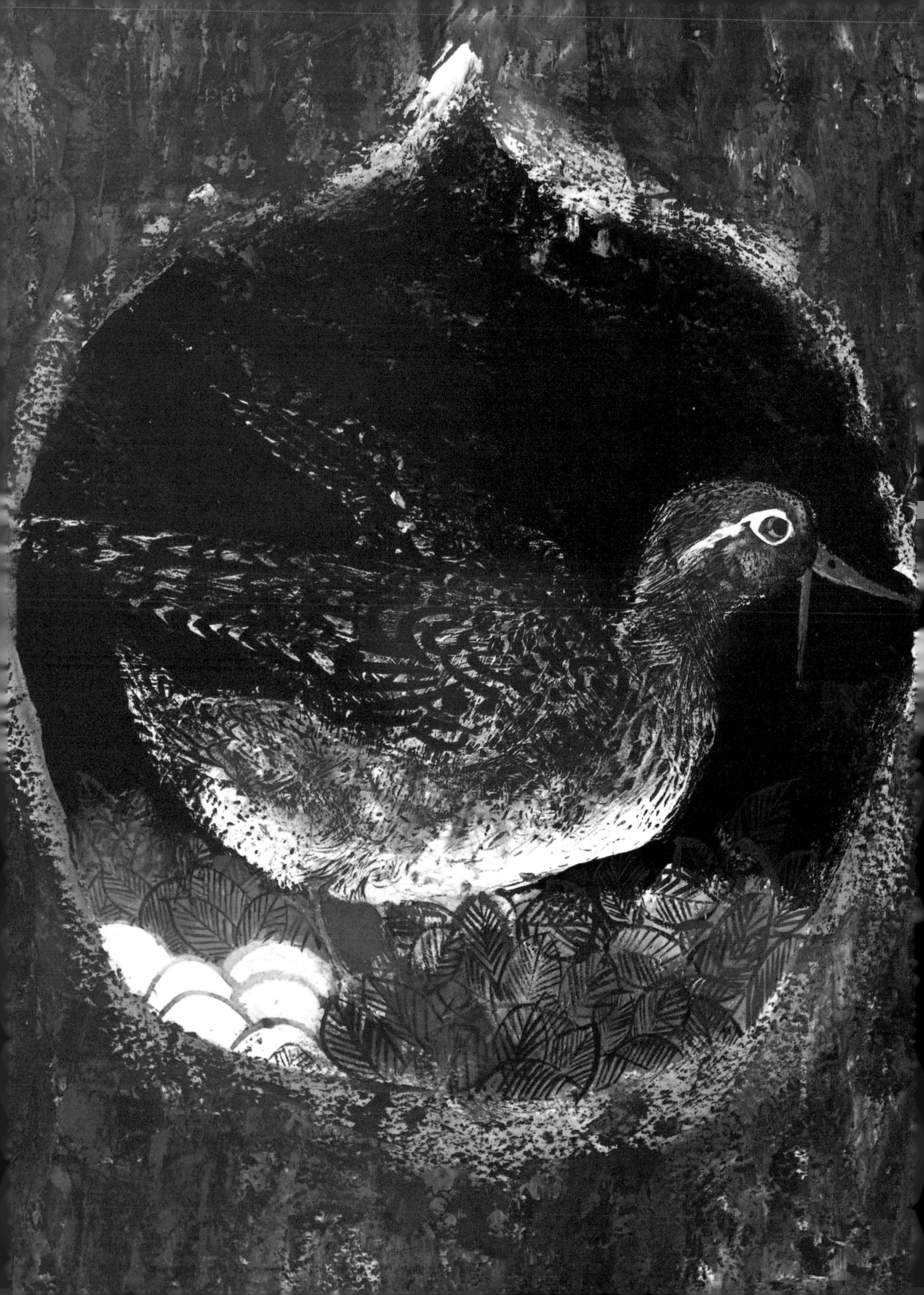

Mother Wood Duck's friends came hurrying
and scurrying to see her eggs.
They were as excited as she was.

"Soon I shall have six beautiful ducklings," she said happily. Then she settled her feathers over the eggs to keep them warm, and she waited.

Day after day Mother Wood Duck sat.

She waited and waited. Every now and then she took a little peek.

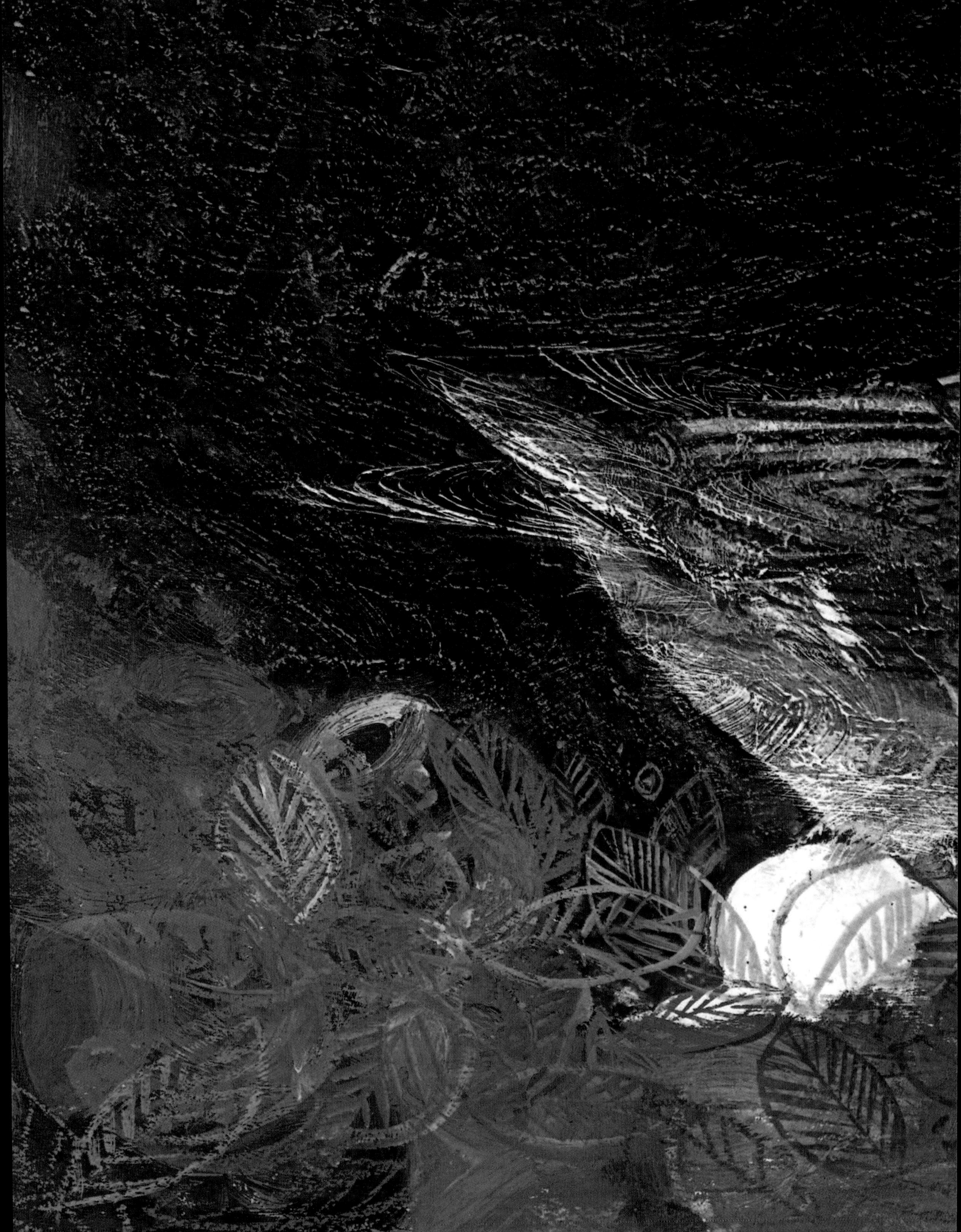

"Perhaps one little duckling is ready to come out," she hoped.

At last, one by one, the little ducklings broke out of their eggs.

Soon they were chasing each other around the tree.

Mother Wood Duck watched over them with pride. She longed for them to be big enough to take their first swim in the lake.

At last, one warm, sunny day, they were ready. Mother Wood Duck called her children. *"Come, dear ducklings,"* she said and led them down to the edge of the lake.

Without a moment's hesitation, the ducklings jumped into the water. They all swam in a nice straight line in and out of the reeds—

—all except the youngest duckling. He swam round and round in a circle, all by himself.

The other ducklings called to him to play, but he just swam round and round.

Every day the ducklings followed their mother into the water. They practiced their swimming, and they learned to dive. But the littlest duckling swam all by himself, round and round in circles. *"He just doesn't want to swim with us,"* complained the other ducklings.

"Come here at once!" Mother Wood Duck cried angrily. *"It is very silly to keep swimming round and round like that."*

"But I can't do it any other way!" wailed the littlest wood duck.

"Nonsense," said the mother duck. *"You are not trying."*

But no matter what his mother said, the little duckling went on swimming in circles. All the other ducklings laughed at him and made rude remarks. The little wood duck was very sad.

"I try and try," he said. *"But I just can't swim any other way."*

The other animals came to watch. Soon they began to tease him. ***"Silly old merry-go-round,"*** shouted the moose.

"I bet you can't even see straight," growled the bear.

Many of the other animals who were watching from the shore laughed and teased him. *"Silly little duck,"* they said. The little wood duck grew sadder and sadder.

Then one day, a wise old owl who was flying past heard the laughter and teasing. He swooped down to see what was happening.

"Little duckling," he called. *"Why are they teasing you?"*

"I can't swim in a straight line. I keep swimming in circles," he explained.

While the little wood duck talked, the owl looked him over carefully.

"Why, young fellow," said the owl. *"You have one foot that is* ***larger*** *than the other. That is why you go round and round. But never mind. There is nothing wrong with swimming in circles. Take no notice of those silly animals."*

Then the owl scolded the other animals for being so unkind and stupid.

A week later, a hungry fox came loping to the lakeside. He stood and watched the ducklings. *"What a fine meal they will make,"* he thought to himself. He waited for the ducklings to come ashore.

But the ducklings hid among the reeds. They were shaking with fright. Only the littlest wood duck kept on swimming.

Round and round he went – faster and faster.

"I'll eat him first," thought the fox. But before long the fox began to feel strange. Watching the duckling swimming round and round and round and round, he began to feel dizzy. It seemed that the grass and the trees and the sky and the lake were all going round and round with the duckling.

"Oh dear!" gasped the fox,
as he fell flat on his back.
He was too dizzy even to sit.

At once, the little ducklings raced home as quickly as they could to their mother.

All the ducklings tried to tell their mother what had happened. All except for the youngest duckling, who stood by modestly.

But his mother felt very proud of him. And all the other ducklings crowded round him to cheer.

"We will never tease you again," they said.

And they never did, for the little wood duck was a hero. He had saved his brothers and sisters. After that, everyone admired his wonderful circles. His brothers and sisters tried to swim in circles, but they could never swim as well as he could.

And the fox, of course,
never, ever came back.